# KUNG FU
# TO THE RESCUE!

adapted by Judy Katschke

Simon Spotlight
New York  London  Toronto  Sydney  New Delhi

SIMON SPOTLIGHT
An imprint of Simon & Schuster Children's Publishing Division
1230 Avenue of the Americas, New York, New York 10020
This Simon Spotlight edition June 2014
Kung Fu Panda Legend of Awesomeness © 2014. Viacom International Inc.
Nickelodeon and all related logos are trademrks of Viacom International Inc.
Based on the featire film "Kung Fu Panda" © 2008 DreamWorks Animation
L.L.C. All rights reserved. All rights reserved, including the right of reproduction in whole or in part in any form. SIMON SPOTLIGHT and colophon are registered trademarks of Simon & Schuster, Inc. For information about special discounts for bulk purchases, please contact Simon & Schuster Special Sales at 1-866-506-1949 or business@simonandschuster.com.
Manufactured in the United States of America 0514 FFG
10 9 8 7 6 5 4 3 2 1
ISBN 978-1-4814-0511-9 (pbk)
ISBN 978-1-4814-0512-6 (hc)
ISBN 978-1-4814-0513-3 (eBook)

# MONKEY IN THE MIDDLE

# CHAPTER **ONE**

**M**onk, old buddy," Po said, his padded panda-paws blocking Monkey's lightning-fast blows. "You picked the wrong sparring partner!"

Monkey broke Po's guard with a powerful back kick. "I know!" he snickered. "But the practice dummy is in the shop!"

"Hy-sterical!" Po smirked. Sure, the Monk-man was a jokester. But this time the joke would be on him!

The Dragon Warrior struck a rock-steady kung-fu pose.

Nothing could break Po's zen-like concentration as he prepared to spar. Nothing but . . .

"Giant rice ball!" Monkey declared.

*Giant . . . rice . . . ball?*

Po's mouth watered like a feng shui fountain. Rice balls were his favorite treats. Besides noodles, dumplings, egg rolls . . .

"What?" Po asked, whipping around.

Monkey grabbed the waistband of Po's pants, yanking it high.

"Urrrrk!" Po howled. The dreaded Blazing Butt Chop was Monkey's signature prank!

"You fall for it every time!" Monkey laughed. "Now I'm going to take you down."

Suddenly—*WHAM*—the gate slammed open. Storming the courtyard was an angry mob of villagers led by Po's dad, Ping!

"Is Shifu at home?" Ping asked. "The angry mob and I must speak with him at once!"

Po was worried. What could be ruffling his dad's feathers? But before he could ask, Shifu, the kung-fu master, walked into the courtyard.

Following him were Masters Crane, Viper, Tigress, Mantis, Monkey, and Po.

"Shifu, you have got to do something!" Ping cried. "The Valley of Peace is being swept by a crime wave."

"Awesome!" Po exclaimed. Then he quickly added, "I meant . . . awesome bad."

Ping flapped his wings as he explained. "The thief even stole my emergency noodle fund!"

Po gulped. The noodle shop? Now it was personal!

"And worse," Ping sobbed. "The thief leaves childish pranks at the scene of each crime!"

Monkey let out an epic gasp.

"Monkey, what's wrong?" Po asked.

"Um . . . nothing," Monkey blurted.

Shifu gave Mr. Ping a reassuring nod. "The Jade Palace will handle this—" he said.

"Hold on, Master Shifu!" Po cut in.

He knew there wasn't a villain the Dragon Warrior and the Furious Five couldn't take on. But this was more than a crime. It was a mystery.

And mysteries—were meant to be *solved*!

# CHAPTER **TWO**

Po was ready for some bodacious case-cracking action. But like all detectives he needed a team. . . .

"Tigress, you'll be my plucky assistant!" Po said.

*Plucky?* Tigress rolled her fierce golden eyes. The only thing she wanted to pluck was a hair from Po's face!

"The Monk-man will be my partner," Po went on. "Like in those buddy-warrior movies."

"Oh, sorry, Po," Monkey said nervously. "But I have . . . other plans."

"That was weird," Mantis said as Monkey raced up the steps to the palace.

Po thought so too. "Monkey loves playing buddy-warrior," he said.

As for Shifu, he wasn't sure about Po's sleuthing

skills. But once he wasn't sure about his kung-fu skills either so . . .

"Mantis, Tigress," Shifu declared. "You'll accompany Po."

*Sweet!* Po thought.

"You won't regret this, Master Shifu," Po said excitedly. "I'll be the best sleuthy, figure-it-out guy the Jade Palace has ever seen!"

Detective Po was on the case. First stop, the crime scene: his dad's noodle shop.

"Plucky assistant, you take notes," Po said, swinging a bamboo stick. "Substitute buddy-warrior, get ready to hold me back when I go berserk!"

Mantis had no idea what Po was

talking about. As for Tigress, she got down to business. . . .

"Mr. Ping, how did the thief get in?" Tigress asked.

"I guard my noodle fund very carefully," Ping explained. "The thief broke in through the locked window."

Po, Tigress, and Mantis saw the window plus some needle-sharp traps on the floor.

"He got past the booby traps!" Ping cried. "And went straight for my secret noodle-fund jar."

"Traps are easy to avoid," Tigress explained. "As long as—"

"Ow! OWIE!"

Ping, Tigress, and Mantis turned to see Po, his paws and chin snapped in traps!

"I'm just getting

inside the head of the thief," Po muttered. Detective work was way harder than he thought. And way more painful!

"Hey!" Mantis called. "Check this out!"

Po shook off the traps to see Mantis holding a patch of fur.

"It must have come off as the thief was making his escape," Tigress declared.

Po knew what to do. He grabbed the fur, sniffed it, then licked it *really* slowly for clues.

"Son, we're wasting time!" Ping complained. "The thief has robbed every merchant on this street except for Wang, the grocer."

"Maybe that's his next target," Mantis said.

"Let's hide across the street and wait for the thief to show," Tigress suggested.

Po's eyes lit up. Secretly waiting for the culprit spelled *stakeout*!

"I call first watch!" Po declared. He sliced the air with a blur of kung-fu chops. "Nothing gets past the Master of Alertness!"

But later, in the dead of night, the Master

of Alertness became the Master of Snooze. . . . Working a stakeout was a lot more tiring than Po thought. His eyelids felt so heavy. . . .

"Po!" Tigress hissed, trying to shake him awake.

"Not without my pants," Po mumbled in his sleep. "Pants . . . come back!"

"The no-pants dream again?" Mantis sighed.

"No!" Po said wide-awake now. "Why would you think that?"

Tigress and Mantis traded smirks. Everyone knew the no-pants dream was Po's worst nightmare.

"Why don't you go splash water on your face?" Tigress suggested. "We have a long night ahead of us."

"Good thinking, plucky assistant." Po smiled. He headed toward the water barrel. But as he splashed water on his face, he heard a noise!

Grabbing his stick, Po peeked into the courtyard. All was still until he spotted a shadowy figure flitting in the dark.

"Halt!" Po shouted, waving his bamboo.

The figure faded from view. Until *POW!* Something hard slammed into Po's face. Po guessed it was a fist.

*"Wah!"* Po cried.

He tried to strike back, but the chain of punches kept flying. Down but not out, Po stood up—only to be bombarded by a hail of apples!

*"Waaaaah!"* Po yelled. As he whirled around to protect himself, he felt two hands grab the

waistband of his pants and pull it up.

"Blazing Butt Chop!" Po wailed, realizing that was Monkey's signature move.

"Hee-hee-hee!" Po's attacker snickered.

As the figure leaped onto a wall, Po noticed a mask covering his attacker's face. Po also noticed long arms and a tail.

Long arms and tail? Sneaky laugh? Blazing Butt Chop? Was his attacker *Monkey*?

# CHAPTER **THREE**

"This can't be happening!" Po said as the shadow jumped out of sight. "Monkey . . . the thief?"

"Or is he?" came a deep voice.

Po looked up. The voice belonged to a pair of pants floating in the air toward him. *His* pants!

"Search your feelings, Po," Pants said. "You know Monkey better than anyone and he's no thief."

"You're right," Po said. "But it sure looked like Monkey."

"Who are you going to believe?" Pants demanded. "Your eyes or your talking pants?"

"Is that a trick question?" Po squeaked. But after listening to Pants, Po had to agree that the attacker couldn't be Monkey.

As Pants vanished, Po had a scary thought. If his pants were up there . . . then . . .

Glancing down, Po sighed with relief. He had on his pants. Now all he needed was evidence that the masked attacker with the Blazing Butt Chop was *not* Monkey!

"So you saw nothing last night?" Shifu asked later.

"Nope!" Po blurted. "And I certainly didn't see anyone we all know personally. Heh, heh. Heh."

How could Po tell anyone about the masked butt-chopper? They would only blame Monkey!

"The only clue we found was this patch of fur," Tigress reported.

Shifu studied the fur in Tigress's claw. "This looks like . . . ape fur," he observed.

"Apes don't have fur." Po forced a laugh.

"I'm pretty sure they do," Tigress said.

Mantis nodded and said, "The only ape around here is—"

"We're wasting time," Po said, snatching Mantis in his paw. "Let's get some sleep!"

"Dude," Mantis said, "you could not be any weirder!"

"Yeeeeah," Po agreed.

But later, while everyone was catching zzz's, Po tiptoed out of his room and down the hall. This time it wasn't for a midnight snack. Detective Po was on a fur-finding mission.

Po stopped in front of Monkey's door. He held up a pair of scissors and said, "Sleep little monkey. Sleep like the wind."

Suddenly the door was opened—by Monkey!

"What are you doing up so late?" Monkey asked nervously.

"Nothing!" Po said quickly. "I'm . . . just going back to my room."

Po waited until Monkey headed down the hall for a drink of water. He then burst into Monkey's room to look for clues.

The first clue Po found was a hunk of Monkey's fur. Licking it lickety-split, Po frowned. This fur matched the piece from the noodle shop. Po was so disappointed.

The next clue was a drawing. It looked like plans of a familiar place.

"The grain mill," Po said slowly. What did the grain mill have to do with Monkey?

The next morning the angry mob returned to the Jade Palace.

"We know who the thief is!" Ping shouted.

"You do?" Monkey gulped.

"I dusted my shop with noodle powder and found these fingerprints on the curtains!" Ping said, presenting the evidence. "They clearly belong to a long-tailed, knuckle-walking monkey!"

"Ping, are you sure?" Shifu asked.

"Noodle powder doesn't lie!" Ping declared.

The angry mob inched toward Monkey. Po had to do something fast!

"Dad, mob, wait!" Po called out. "Fine, Monkey's fingerprints and fur were at the crime scene—"

"Po," Monkey cut in.

"Sure, the thief I saw last night had a long tail and moved like a monkey," Po added.

"You saw the thief last night?" Tigress demanded.

"You didn't say anything!" Shifu scolded.

Po kept on defending Monkey. He was a great master, warrior, and best friend, but most of all . . .

"He's no thief!" Po insisted. "Right, Monkey? Tell them the truth!"

"I *am* the thief," Monkey said.

Po couldn't believe his ears. Was Monkey going bananas, or did he just admit to being the thief?

"Monkey, no!" Po groaned.

"Get him!" shouted a villager. As the angry mob charged toward Monkey, the Furious Five stepped forward.

As Monkey performed a backflip, he kicked the Furious Five out of the way. He then shot away from the palace and the mob.

"We must pursue Monkey at once!" Shifu said.

Just then Po remembered the grain mill.

"I think I know where Monkey's headed!" Po said. "Let me go alone. He'll listen to me!"

Shifu didn't know whether to trust Po, especially after Po protected a thief who stole from his own father!

"I hope Monkey listens to you," Shifu said firmly. "Because if he doesn't, we'll be coming for both of you."

Po gulped at the not-so-bodacious thought. He then dashed out of the palace.

When Po reached the grain mill, he

peeked inside. There was the mill with its massive wheel and grinding stones. And there was Monkey—standing over a pot and counting gold coins!

"Monkey, listen," Po said gently. "I don't know why you're doing this, but I won't let you throw away our friendship!"

Monkey's eyes burned through his mask at Po. Then without warning—*WHAM! WHAM! WHAM!* Po saw stars as Monkey riddled him with forward strikes!

Through it all, Po grabbed Monkey's tail. He swung Monkey around and around before swinging him onto the ground. Monkey grunted as Po sat on him with a *THUMP*!

Po yanked off Monkey's mask. But the face underneath was not Monkey's!

"Who are you?" Po cried.

"He's my brother, Wukong," a voice replied.

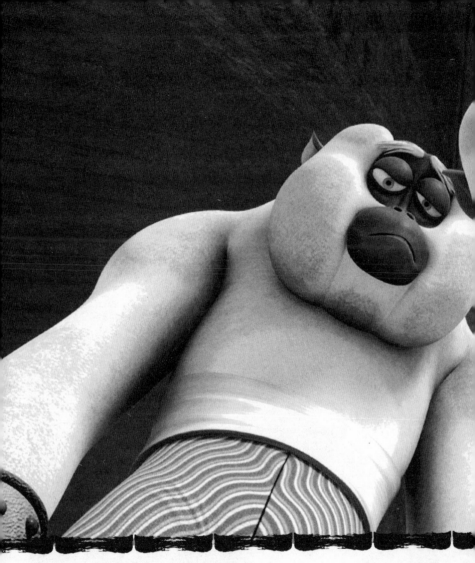

It was Monkey's voice! Po turned to see his friend standing right behind him.

"Your brother!" Po said, relieved. "I knew it wasn't—*Waaaaaah!!!*"

Po's eyes rolled until he slumped to the ground.

Monkey had knocked him out with a paralyzing
nerve punch!

Wukong jumped to his feet and laughed.

"Nighty-night, panda!"

# CHAPTER **FOUR**

Po opened his eyes to find his hands chained to the wall. He was happy to see Monkey until he remembered who knocked him out cold!

"Monkey, I know he's your brother," Po said. "But why are you protecting this chump?"

Monkey heaved a sigh. He told Po the story of two brothers who loved playing pranks but later chose very different paths. Monkey trained at the Jade Palace. Wukong sunk into a life of crime to become the notorious King of Thieves.

"Our mother loved Wukong dearly," Monkey explained, "and made me swear to protect the family."

That's when Po got it. Monkey didn't want to break his promise to his mother.

"That's my brother, and he may be a sap"— Wukong guffawed—"but I can always count on his protection!"

Po gritted his teeth with rage. So that's what this was all about: Wukong was putting the blame on Monkey!

"You're going down, Wukong!" Po shouted as he broke though his chains.

"Uh-oh." Wukong gulped. But before he could strike Po, he was blocked by the handle of a pitchfork. Holding it was Monkey!

Po pleaded with Monkey to turn his brother in, but Monkey refused.

"I made a vow to my mother!" Monkey shouted. He dropped the pitchfork and struck Po. Po struck back, pinning Monkey against the wall.

"Monkey!" Po cried. "Don't make me—"

*WHAM!*

A chop from behind knocked Po out cold.

"Who's the chump now, chump?" Wukong snapped.

He took the passed-out panda and hurled him toward the mill. Monkey watched in horror as his

friend landed on the conveyer belt, moving toward the perilous grinding stones!

"Po!" Monkey cried. He tried to pull Po off, but Wukong's combat moves made it impossible.

"I've always had the moves on you," Wukong jeered.

"I've been practicing a little since then," Monkey said, showing off his kung-fu skills.

The fight moved on top of the wheel. As it spun, Wukong wrapped Monkey's foot with a chain. Using his free hand, Monkey struck Wukong off the wheel. As Wukong landed on Po, Po snapped awake. Now both were riding the belt toward the perilous grinding stones!

Monkey jumped down from the wheel. He knocked Wukong and Po out of harm's way, only to get his chain wrapped in the grinder.

"Monkey!" Po shouted. But before his friend could become mutilated monkey meat, an arm appeared from above.

"Hold on, bro!" a voice shouted.

Po and Monkey glanced up. Hanging over the grinder by his tail was Wukong!

Wukong grabbed Monkey's hand, pulling him way up. Po thought the brothers were safe, until Wukong's tail slipped, sending both tumbling toward the grinder!

"Hi-yaaaaaa!" the Dragon Warrior cried, grabbing a nearby log and smashing the grinding stones to smithereens.

As the mill caved in, Po snatched the brothers midair and carried them to safety. But Monkey wasn't safe from the angry mob storming the ruins. . . .

"There he is!" Ping shouted, pointing to Monkey.

"He's not the thief!" Wukong declared. "I am!"

The surprised villagers listened as Wukong confessed. Po was proud of Wukong for taking full responsibility for the crimes.

"There's just one thing I'd like to say in my defense," Wukong added.

"What's that?" Po asked.

"Is that a giant rice ball?" Wukong asked.

*Rice ball?* Po turned only to feel his pants being yanked up by Wukong!

"So long losers!" The King of Thieves laughed as he scrambled away.

"Blazing Butt Chop!" Po groaned. "I fall for it every time!"

But yanked pants were better than no pants. And everyone in the Valley of Peace was super-proud of their Dragon Warrior. Po had stopped the crime wave and hopefully someday Wukong!

"I hope I never see another crazy, thieving, practical-joke-playing monkey again!" Po told Monkey later as they cleaned up the mill.

"Rice ball!" Monkey shouted.

Po chuckled. As if he would fall for *that* trick again. But Monkey had more tricks up his furry sleeve. He tugged a string and—*SPLAT*—sticky white paint from a bucket poured all over Po!

"Hee-hee-hee!" Monkey giggled.

Po had to smile too. Monkey wasn't a thief, but he would always be a prankster. And he would always be an awesomely awesome *friend*!

# CRANE ON A WIRE

# CHAPTER **ONE**

If there was anything Po loved more than kung fu and dumplings, it was telling a good story:

"Legend tells of the awesomely awesome giant, Charitable Chan. . . ."

The Furious Five was all ears as Po told the tale of his favorite hero, the giant panda who sought out the rich, giving their shiny coins to those in need.

"Da, da, da, daaaaaaah!" Po sang as he rattled a pot filled with coins.

Like Charitable Chan, Po was collecting for the children's hospital. The Furious Five knew a good cause when they heard one, so Tigress, Monkey, Mantis, and Viper each dropped a coin into the pot. But when it came to Crane . . .

"Sorry, Po," Crane said. "I spent my last few coins on a new nasal irrigator."

Crane held up a squeeze bottle used to suck out stuffy noses.

"But I'd be happy to donate my services in any way I can!" Crane said before clearing his nose with a loud *HONK*!

Po's eyes lit up. His allergic bud had given him the most awesome idea!

"We can *all* donate our services!" Po suggested. "We'll hold an auction. Whoever bids the most gets to spend the day with their favorite kung-fu master!"

Monkey hated the idea. What if Mrs. Yoon bid on him? She smelled like paste!

"Where's your furious feistiness?" Po demanded. "You guys are just ssss-cared that you'll get ssss-moked!" Po teased that he would make the most money since he was the most popular kung-fu master.

The Furious Five glared at Po. Who was he calling ssss-cared and ssss-moked?

One by one the Furious Five agreed, and the Jade Palace Fancy-Pants Auction was *on*!

"Another victory for Charitable Chan!" Po cheered. "Da, da, da, daaaaaaah!"

The auction was set up in a flash. Almost everyone in the Valley of Peace gathered in the square to bid for their favorite kung-fu master. . . .

"First up," Ping announced from the stage. "Master Tigress!"

Tigress shot up high in the air. She scissored her legs, chopping airborne blocks of wood with her feet. The blocks landed on the ground in a perfect pagoda!

"Twenty yuan!" the villagers bid.

"Twenty-five!"

"Thirty!"

"Forty!"

"Sold for forty!" Ping said, pointing to a family of bunnies. "You win a day with Tigress!"

Next was Monkey's turn. Everyone oohed and aahed as he balanced on his tail, juggling plates in the air. As the plates dropped, Monkey chopped them into teeny-tiny pieces!

"Fifty!" a voice bid.

"Fifty yuan wins a day with Monkey!" Ping declared.

When Monkey saw the bidder, he gulped. It was smelly Mrs. Yoon!

"You've got a hard act to follow, Crane." Po smiled.

"Oh yeah?" Crane smiled back. "Just watch!"

Spreading his wings, Crane rocketed into the air. He touched down and said, "Hi-yaaa! Hi-yaaa," while he sliced boards in half with his speedy, spindly feet.

The crowd was mystified by Crane's kung-fu ease . . . until he let out a huge wet sneeze!

"Ew," a little bunny said.

As Crane kept honking, his price kept dropping.

"Come on, people!" Po urged. "This is Master Crane we're talking about!"

But Crane was a no-sale. Especially when everyone saw his nasal irrigator.

"Sorry I ruined your auction, Po." Crane sighed.

Po watched as Crane headed sadly back to the palace. He felt bad for his friend, but the auction had to go on.

"Let's keep the good times rolling with the Dragon Warrior!" Ping declared.

Po struck a fierce kung-fu pose. But just as he was about to perform some excellent moves— *BOOM!*

A murky shadow loomed over the square. Everyone looked up to see a dark-spirited owl, hovering above the square!

"Fenghuang!" Tigress declared.

The steel-eyed villain cackled evilly. "You didn't think that pathetic cage could hold me," she sneered. "Did you?"

# CHAPTER **TWO**

"She's going to attack!" Monkey shouted.

Like a fighter plane, Fenghuang crashed into a building. It crumbled to the ground, all over Po and the Furious Five!

When Crane heard screams, he hurried back to the square. Staring at the rubble, he gulped. "Po? Tigress? What happened?"

"I'll be happy to show you!" Fenghuang shouted.

With needle-sharp talons, Fenghuang lifted Crane into the air. She spun him around and around before smashing the dizzy bird into a building—beak first!

Po poked his head out from the rubble. When he saw Fenghuang zooming toward him, he held up an iron wok. Fenghuang flew closer and closer until—*WHAM*—her talons rammed painfully into Po's shield.

When Po saw Fenghuang's twisted talons, he grinned. "You guys!" he said. "Her talons can't cut through iron!"

Fenghuang's secret was out. The Furious Five had a field day blocking and attacking the owl with iron bars and bolts.

"My beautiful talons!" Fenghuang moaned.

Madder than ever, Fenghuang soared back for more until Po sent her flying with a bouncing belly bump!

"Hi-yaaaaa!" Po cried.

The villagers cheered as their feathered foe flew off with twisted talons and a broken wing.

"Let's hear it for the Dragon Warrior," Ping declared. "And the Furious Five!"

"More like the Furious *Four*," another duck said. He pointed to Crane. His beak was still jammed into the wall.

"I'm okay," Crane muttered as the villagers laughed.

Po knew Crane had to sharpen his kung-fu skills. But back at the palace, Crane's skills turned into embarrassing spills. Even the punching bag punched back!

65

"My life's a lie," Crane groaned. "The people I've sworn to protect think I'm a joke."

Po tried to change Crane's image with a fashion makeover. But when Crane worked his color-splashed hat and Fu Manchu mustache, the villagers laughed again!

"Face it. I'm a joke!" Crane said.

Viper, Monkey, Tigress, and Mantis weren't laughing. They had spotted Fenghuang high in the mountains nursing her broken wing.

"This is our chance to capture her!" Tigress said excitedly. "We've got to get up there while she's still weak."

"I'm not going," Crane said.

"Crane, we need you!" Po insisted.

"Po, you saw me freeze up when Fenghuang attacked today," Crane argued. "You heard every-one laughing too!"

"Po, he's made his choice," Tigress said. "We've got to get going."

There was no time to waste. Soon, Po and the others were scaling the snowy mountainside to reach Fenghuang.

"Come to me!" Fenghuang sneered, spying from above. She waited until her foes settled on a ledge. Then using her good wing, she sent chunks of rock tumbling below.

"Rockslide!" Monkey shouted.

A humongous boulder crashed down between Tigress and the others. It was a trap! Fenghuang swooped down toward Tigress, her talons protected with iron gloves.

Po tried to help Tigress, but he couldn't reach her. Tigress put up a good fight, but her skills were no match for Fenghuang's armored talons.

With one deadly swipe, the vengeful owl sent
Tigress tumbling over the icy ledge!

"Tigress!" Po shouted as he watched his friend
tumble down the mountainside. "Noooooo!"

# CHAPTER **THREE**

Tigress thought she was a goner as she plummeted toward the ground, until a save by Monkey's long arm stopped her fall.

"Got you!" Monkey declared.

Po and the others formed a lifeline to keep from falling. When Fenghuang

saw it, she brandished her talons, slashing the lifeline apart. Next she soared to the mountaintop
where she sent down a powerful snowy avalanche.

"It's over, panda!" Fenghuang shouted.

Meanwhile down in the peaceful valley, Crane swept the courtyard with his friend Zeng.

"Why didn't you go with the others, Master Crane?" Zeng asked.

"Because I'm a joke, Zeng," Crane replied.

A loud rumble filled the air. Crane and Zeng looked up to see snow cascading down the mountainside.

"Shouldn't we do something?" Zeng gasped.

A horrified Crane watched as tons of snow poured down. Po . . . Tigress . . . Mantis . . .

"What do we do, Master Crane?" Zeng asked. "What do we do?"

# CHAPTER **FOUR**

Po and his friends dragged themselves out of the fallen snow. The wicked owl thought it was a hoot—especially when Tigress began clawing up the mountainside.

"Kitty still wants to play?" Fenghuang sneered. She soared off the mountaintop to attack Tigress. Po jumped to the rescue, grabbing onto Fenghuang's feet.

"Gotcha!" Po said.

But for Fenghuang it was game on. She spread
her wings, taking Po on a sky-high joy ride.

"Mama!" Po gulped as they rose higher and
higher. The thin air made him dizzy and weak. So
weak he finally lost his grip.

"Scratch one Dragon Warrior!" Fenghuang laughed as Po dropped through the air toward the ground.

Po groaned as he saw a giant panda-patty in his future. But his luck was about to change because flying to the rescue was another kung-fu warrior. It was Crane!

Crane swooped under Po, planting his feet on a bamboo stick. Then the two soared straight toward Fenghuang!

"No!" Fenghuang cried when she saw Po.

"Up, up, and in your face!" Po shouted.

Po was on a roll. He struck Fenghuang with a series
of forward strikes. Then with a masterful airborne flip,
the Dragon Warrior sent Fenghuang flying!

"This is very bad for sinuses!" Crane honked.

Po and Crane thought they saw the last of
Fenghuang until she returned to knock Po off his
bamboo perch.

"Double gie!" Po groaned as he tumbled toward the ground. The villagers gasped as the panda landed flat on his face.

"Po, come on!" Crane shouted down. "I can't defeat her by myself!"

"What's the matter, little birdie?" Fenghuang taunted. "Lost your confidence?"

Crane bristled at the owl's sinister laugh. He was sick of being a joke. He was an accomplished kung-fu master with an important job: to protect the Valley of Peace from evil. Evil creeps like Fenghuang!

"I just found
my confidence!" Crane declared.

The battle of the birds raged
from a talon-biting chase through a
bamboo forest to claw-to-claw combat
in the village square.

"Ooh! Aah!" the villagers gasped.

Feathers flew as Fenghuang swiped at Crane.
With a swift move Crane grabbed Fenghuang by
the feet, hurling her down a deep, craggy chimney.
Moments later the owl staggered out, eyes rolling inside her head. Everyone waited breathlessly

until a dazed Fenghuang fell flat on her face!

"Crane, you did it!" Po said excitedly. "You beat Fenghuang!"

"Mas-ter Crane!" the villagers cheered. "Mas-ter Crane!"

Crane grinned as he felt the love. Not only were his kung-fu skills back—he was a hero.

And *that* was nothing to sneeze at!

HERE'S A SNEEK PEAK AT ANOTHER EXCITING **KUNG FU PANDA:** LEGENDS OF AWESOMENESS TALE!

THE FU

THE FU

# CHAPTER ONE

"Taste the sting of my steel!" grunted a rhino captain as he slammed his playing piece down on a game board.

"Nice move, Chief," said his opponent, a rhino guard.

They were watching over a bridge on the Chinese border . . . but it was a quiet night.

Then a stone tumbled down from the rocky cliffs behind them, and the two rhinos looked up. A small emperor tamarin monkey with a white beard was bounding across the bridge toward them.

"Border patrol! Identify yourself!" demanded the captain.

"Fools! You are like worms challenging a large dog or perhaps a midsized cow," said the monkey, his voice full of contempt. "You are helpless before me—Pai Mei, high priest of Abusive Lotus!"

He struck a kung-fu pose.

"Pai Mei? Wasn't he that traitor who tried to destroy the emperor?" the guard asked.

"Get him!" yelled the captain.

They charged at Pai Mei, pointing their spears at him, but the little monkey backflipped out of the way. Then he kicked the spears out of the rhinos' hands and posed again, holding his paws in front of him. They glowed white with mysterious energy.

*Pow! Pow!* He struck each rhino once in the chest, and the great beasts toppled over, groaning.

"Now, you unworthy soapmongers, direct me to the kung-fu master known as Shifu," Pai Mei demanded.

"Shifu?" the captain replied, his voice shaking with fear. "He's in the Valley of Peace."

Pai Mei grinned, satisfied. "He shall be my next miserable victim," he said, and then leaped away.

"Next victim?" the captain asked, puzzled, turning to the guard. They both looked down to the spot where Pai Mei's glowing paw had touched them, which was glowing with white heat.

*BOOM!*

A blast sent the rhinos flying off the bridge, into the valley below.

"Ugh," the two rhinos groaned.

So much for a quiet night.